Chrissy—

Thank you!

Melanie Brazdzi

MIRANDA MOOSE LOVES ORANGE JUICE

written by
Melanie Brazdzionis

illustrations by
Ning Loo

Author - Melanie Brazdzionis

Illustrator - Ning Loo

Editor - Amanda Bidnall

Designer - Sunny Duran

First edition:
ISBN 979-8-9880460-0-4 (hardcover)
ISBN 979-8-9880460-1-1 (paperback)
ISBN 979-8-9880460-2-8 (ebook)

For Luke and Kelly
~M.B.

For Ma, Pa, Feng and Yu
~ N. L.

Our story begins with a moose in the wood,
Who does not always behave in the way that she should.
Her forest companions would never have guessed
That she'd leave them all to follow her quest.
In the pages that follow, I'm compelled to report,
Her new neighbors are of a different sort ...

Meet Miss Miranda Mae Meredith Moose.

Our Miss Miranda just **LOVES** orange juice.

She's fond of soda pops flavored with cherries.
She enjoys most juice from freshly squeezed berries.
Miss Moose thinks coffee and tea are OK...
but most of all, she must have her OJ!

One sunny morning, while making her bed,
she's dreaming of gooseberry jam on her bread.

She wanders downstairs and then peeks in the fridge—
but there's no juice at all, not even a smidge!

She dresses at once, and she runs to the store ...

only to discover the store has no more!

What's a moose to do when she's out of **OJ**,
and she can't live without it for even a day?!

"I'll visit the farm where my neighbors live.
Perhaps one of them has some juice they can give."

Our moose finds her little friend, Miss Hallie Hen,
shooing her chicks away from the pig pen.
"Oh tweedle-dee-dee, Miranda, my dear,
unfortunately, there's no orange juice here."

"I have dozens of eggs, and a few bits of grain,
but perhaps you should try Cassie Cow, down the lane."

Miranda says thank you and goes on her way,
hoping Miss Cow has a tad of **OJ**.

"Oh *noooo*, Miss Miranda," Miss Cassie Cow utters.
"I only have milks and sweet creamery butters.
But try asking Shelly. She's helpful and caring.
She even loves sharing whatever she's wearing!"

"Thank you, Miss Cassie!" cries Miranda Moose,
now bursting with thirst in her quest for more juice.

She crosses the meadow and finds little Shelly,
quietly grazing and filling her belly.

"Hello, Miss Sheep! I've been uphill and down;
I've asked Mr. Goat, Hallie Hen, and Miss Cow."
(She pauses to wipe off the sweat from her brow.)
"Now, at long last, I am here to inquire;
might you have the sweet orange juice I desire?"

"I'd give you the wool off my *baa-baa-baa-baack*,
if that's what you need, if that's what you lack.
But orange juice? I'm so sorry, Miss Moose,
that's something a sheep does **NOT** produce."

"Hmm ...

I do have a friend, and perhaps you have met her...
she has some juice—and there is no juice better!
Walk down the path to see Mrs. O'Tree.
She'll help you for sure if it's **OJ** you need."

"Why in the world would an old **TREE** drink juice?
It just cannot be," says the baffled Miss Moose.

"Just go," says Shelly. "You're in for a treat!"
Then her curly head rests, and she falls right to sleep.

Our weary Miranda follows Shelly's direction.
She treks up the trail without asking a question.

Over hill and dale until the path unwinds...
When suddenly, you won't believe what she finds.

At the edge of the forest, near her very own front door,
stands a fruit tree she's never noticed before!

Miranda's eyes grow as wide as the skies.
Now, what do you think is her biggest surprise?

Mrs. O'Tree has orange juice aplenty!

Why **WOULD** a moose think a tree wouldn't have any?